Rarity's Charity

Little, Brown and Company
Hachette Book Group
1290 Avenue of the Americas, New York, NY 10104
Visit us at LBYR.com
mylittlepony.com

First published as *My Little Pony: Rarity and the Curious Case of Charity* by Little, Brown and Company in April 2014;
Originally adapted in 2017 by Five Mile, an imprint of Bonnier Publishing Australia in Australia.
First U.S. Edition: November 2019

Little, Brown and Company is a division of Hachette Book Group, Inc. The Little, Brown name and logo are trademarks of Hachette Book Group, Inc.

Library of Congress Control Number 2013034583

ISBNs: 978-0-316-49297-3 (pbk.), 978-0-316-49299-7 (ebook)

Printed in the United States of America

LSC-C

10 9 8 7 6 5 4 3 2 1

Licensed By:

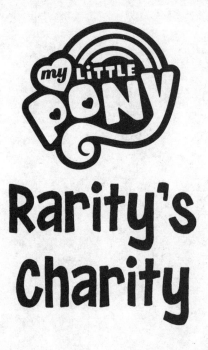

Rarity's Charity

G. M. Berrow

LITTLE, BROWN AND COMPANY
NEW YORK ✳ BOSTON

Chapter 1

Rarity is waiting for a letter confirming her acceptance into the House of Outrageous and Opulent Fashion (H.O.O.F.) Summer Mentor Program to arrive. She applied to be a mentor months ago but hasn't heard a peep since then.

Rarity glances out the window at the mailbox.

"I must stop watching the mail," she tells herself. "This order for the Ponyville Choir is far more work than I thought it would be. Fifteen dresses, and bow ties for the stallions, too! What in Equestria was I thinking?"

If only Rarity had the helping hoof of

an apprentice, everything would go much faster. She could never admit to the other ponies that she was falling behind.

Suddenly, she notices the mail pony flying past. Rarity races outside at once!

"*Mmmmf umph mrrfff, ump ferf,*" the mail pony mumbles, before dropping a purple envelope from her mouth and flying off.

"Excusez-moi?" Rarity calls after

the mail pony. "What was that, darling?"

Rarity's little sister, Sweetie Belle, trots over to pick it up.

"She said sorry for losing the letter. She knows you must have been waiting for it," Sweetie Belle explains, handing Rarity the letter.

Rarity examines the envelope and lets out a squeal. She recognizes the H.O.O.F. crest. "'To the illustrious Rarity of Ponyville,'" she reads. "'We are honored to welcome you into one

of the most exclusive societies in
Equestrian fashion: the H.O.O.F.
Mentors!'"

"Yay!" Sweetie Belle jumps up and
down.

Rarity reads on: "'You will soon be joined by your new apprentice, Sweetmint, a student from Larsons The Neigh School for Design, and—'" Suddenly, the smile falls from Rarity's face. "Oh no!"

"What?" Sweetie Belle cries. "What is it, Rarity?"

"This is a disaster!" Rarity clutches her hooves to her chest. "She arrives tomorrow!"

Chapter 2

The next day, Rarity feels so lucky that her best friends have come with her to the train station to pick up her mentee. Pinkie Pie, Applejack, Fluttershy, Princess Twilight Sparkle,

Rainbow Dash, and Spike always make things extra special.

"This is so exciting, Rarity!" says Twilight Sparkle. "Your very own student." Twilight loves everything to do with learning.

"Does sound kinda nice," Applejack chimes in. "Sometimes I think I could use a little more help around the farm."

"I'm not hosting her because I need *help*," Rarity replies defensively. "It's about giving back to Equestria."

Applejack glances at her. "How do you figure that?"

"I'm giving back to the community that made me. I am going to guide an up-and-comer through the daunting— yet rewarding—fashion industry." Rarity puffs up with pride. "Now hurry along!" she adds. It would be awful if Sweetmint were standing on the empty train platform alone.

"Ponyville Station!" hollers the conductor stallion as the train comes to a stop at the station.

A stream of exotic ponies begin exiting the train cars.

"Do you know what she looks like?" asks Twilight, craning her neck.

"I haven't the slightest idea," answers Rarity anxiously. "Could she be that one in the hat there?" Rarity points her hoof at a tall, willowy pony sporting a purple

hat with feathers. "No, probably not."
Feathers are very last year.

"Just relax," Twilight reassures her.
"We'll find her."

"You're right," Rarity says.
Everypony knows who Rarity is. The
society pages have been littered with
pictures of elite ponies wearing her
fashions.

"Who's that?" asks Spike, pointing
at a young Unicorn with a striking

resemblance to Rarity. She has a white coat, a pale-green mane and tail, and a cutie mark of three light-blue heart-shaped gems. A dark-green scarf is expertly draped around her neck, and she is clearly looking for somepony. It has to be her.

Chapter 3

"That's her!" exclaims Rarity, prancing toward the newcomer. "You must be Sweetmint from Manehattan," she says. "Welcome to Ponyville!"

The Unicorn squeals. "Oh, Rarity!

Wow! It's really you!" Her big eyes widen. "But how did you know what I looked like?"

"I spied your utterly fabulous scarf," explains Rarity, sizing her up. "Only a true fashionista would know that forest green is the color of the moment!"

Sweetmint shakes her head in disbelief. "I can't believe it's actually you!"

"Oh, stop, darling!" Rarity flips her mane and laughs. Then she waves the pony on with a grin. "No, please continue if you must, Sweetmint."

"Oh, actually…um…it's Charity, actually. H.O.O.F. must have used my, uh, nickname or something," she says, looking around nervously.

Pinkie Pie pipes up. "Hey, your names are almost the same!"

"Oh, I didn't introduce you!" exclaims Rarity. "Charity, please meet Rainbow Dash, Applejack, Fluttershy, Pinkie Pie, and Her Grand Royal

Highness Princess Twilight Sparkle."
Rarity is very proud of being friends
with royalty. "They're my very best
friends in the whole world."

Charity bows her head. "What an
honor!"

"Shall we?" Rarity motions toward
the station's exit. "Spike, can you take
the luggage, please?"

But the Dragon is completely
mesmerized by Charity. Spike doesn't
seem to hear the request as he stares at

the new pony's mane; Rarity has to clear her throat to snap him out of his daze. Blushing, Spike scrambles to grab the biggest suitcase.

Charity giggles. "Thank you, sir."

"At your service, miss." Spike bows.

Charity lowers her voice and whispers to Rarity, "I sure hope everypony likes me."

"Don't worry, dear," Rarity assures her. "If you're anything like me, we'll all become fast friends!"

Chapter 4

Later that afternoon, Charity looks around the boutique while Rarity makes tea. "Wow! Now, this is a real designer's workshop. Nothing like *my* apartment."

The room is littered with bolts of fabric, and the model ponnequins are outfitted in matching green dresses. The fabric is expertly draped and pinned, but they're still far from completion.

Charity examines the half-clothed ponnequins. "Oh, this fabric is totally gorgeous! Very John Gallopiano."

"Those outfits are for the Ponyville Choir. They have a concert coming up," Rarity explains as she fills a pair of teacups. "But I detest what I've created. If I had time, I'd start over." Rarity looks at the ponnequins wistfully. "Alas, every artist must go through their process."

"What's your process?" Charity asks.

"Oh, my process is always changing." Rarity's current process is denial. The Ponyville Choir concert is next week and her outfits aren't ready! But right now, she feels she must focus on her new apprentice. She's sure everything will fall into place.

"Now, enough about me." Rarity takes the seat across from Charity and sips her tea. "Bluedazzle berry tart? They're my favorite!" She nudges a plate with the tarts toward her apprentice.

"Oh, I just *love* Bluedazzle berries!" But Charity takes only a teensy bite then pushes her plate away.

Rarity glances down at the H.O.O.F. program brochure. "Tell me about this fabulous H.O.O.F. fashion competition."

Charity takes a sip of tea. "Well, each apprentice presents the line they worked on with their mentor. The winner gets to display their designs in the fall windows at Sacks."

Sacks is one of the biggest, fanciest

department stores in Manehattan. Having displays in their windows would be unbelievable exposure for Charity's designs!

"You don't seem thrilled about that, dear," says Rarity, looking at Charity's glum face. "It's Sacks, for Celestia's sake!"

"But all the ponies in my program are so talented; there's no way I'll ever win!" Charity explains.

"Oh, that attitude simply won't do!"
Rarity says. "Stick with me, Charity.
You'll be in the spotlight in no time."

Chapter 5 ✷

"**I**s there anything you need me to do?" Charity asks once they've finished their tea. She trots over to the choir dresses and begins riffling through them. "I could work on this for you. Maybe alter the hem and bring the sleeves up a bit?"

"NO!" Rarity shouts. "Get your hooves off!"

Charity drops a gown in shock. "Sorry, I—"

"No, *I'm* sorry, darling." Rarity laughs nervously. "I'm just very protective of my work. You understand?"

"Of course,"

Charity says, nodding.

Rarity glances at the H.O.O.F. brochure on the table.

"Maybe we should start working on your fashion line!" Rarity exclaims. She loves starting new projects.

"Now?" Charity asks, looking around at all the unfinished choir dresses.

"No time like the present to make today a beautiful gift," Rarity says with purpose. She knows she should be working on the choir costumes. But she also wants to help Charity. Rarity clears her throat. "First, you need to come up with an extraordinary topic."

Charity bites her lip. "How do you do that?"

"I always look at my surroundings," Rarity says. They look around the messy workshop. There are fabric scraps, sewing tools, and a heap of unfinished choir dresses.

"How about a line inspired by...

spools of thread?" suggests Charity.

Rarity frowns. "Let's keep thinking.

It'll come together. Remember: When

the going gets tough, the tough get

sewing!"

"Hello? Is anypony here?" calls a

soft voice from the front of the

boutique.

"Duty calls!" Rarity says, quickly

trotting out of the room.

Chapter 6

Fluttershy has come to the boutique to invite Rarity and Charity to a picnic. Twilight Sparkle, Applejack, Rainbow Dash, and Pinkie Pie will all be there as well.

"What am I going to wear?" Charity squeals when Fluttershy has left.

"I was wondering the exact same thing," says Rarity. "What have you brought from Manehattan?"

Charity unpacks, and soon expensive clothes surround the ponies. Rarity notices a one-shouldered gown made of light-green, willowy organza. She's never seen anything like it.

"Who designed this impeccable piece?" Rarity asks in wonder as she admires the exquisite beadwork.

Charity quickly snatches it away. "Oh, that's just something I ... found." She tosses the dress back into a suitcase.

Rarity is confused. "But where did—" Rarity begins to ask.

"Oh, what about this?" Charity interrupts, holding up a glittery sun hat. "I just bought it at Neighcy's and it's—"

"A Rarity original!" Rarity can't believe it.

"I found your matching one in the closet. I hope you don't mind." Charity puts the second hat on Rarity's head and giggles. "We'll be just like twins!"

Rarity looks in the mirror. If it weren't for her green mane, Charity *could* be her twin.

"What do you think?" Charity looks hopeful. "Can I pull it off?"

Rarity smiles. "Absolutely, darling."

✳ Chapter 7 ✳

When Rarity and Charity arrive, the picnic is in full swing. Applejack and Rainbow Dash are doing cannonballs into the lake.

"We've arrived!" Rarity announces.

"I'm so glad you could make it," Twilight says, smiling.

"Hi, Charity!" Spike yells a bit too enthusiastically. Rarity shoots him a look. "Oh, and—uh—you, too, Rarity. You're looking nice today," he quickly adds as an afterthought.

"Thank you, Spike," Rarity replies. "We're very busy today, but time with friends does wonders for creativity." Rarity puts on her sunglasses. "So I thought this would simply be the perfect distraction!"

"Um, indeed," Charity echoes, nodding. "Simply perfect."

Twilight raises an eyebrow at the posh accent Charity is putting on.

Applejack trots over, dripping wet from her last cannonball. "Good to have ya here, Charity!" She tips her cowpony hat. "Care to join in our little contest, girls?"

"*Oooh!*" Charity exclaims, taking off her own hat.

Rarity wrinkles her nose. "I refuse to mess up this look with murky lake water. But you go ahead, Charity."

"No, you're right," Charity says quickly. She pulls her hat back on. "Lake water is disgusting."

"Are you sure, Charity?" asks Twilight Sparkle. "It seems like you wanted to try it."

"Nope, I'm good!" Charity replies, before quickly correcting herself. "I mean—no, thank you, darling."

Twilight frowns. It's clear that Charity is learning something from her mentor—maybe too much.

✦ Chapter 8 ✦

Rarity leans back in her deck chair and closes her eyes. The warmth of the sunshine on her face is just *glorious*. Just as she starts to doze off, somepony interrupts her.

"How are things going with you and Charity?" asks Twilight.

Rarity opens one eye to see Twilight standing next to her expectantly. "Things are going great," Rarity replies. "We have so much in common!"

"It certainly seems that way," Twilight says with concern.

"What does that mean?" Rarity sits up.

"I just worry that Charity is taking

her admiration for you a little too far."
Twilight shrugs.

"I have no idea what you're talking about," says Rarity. "She's a classy, sophisticated pony."

Before Twilight can respond, Rarity suddenly shrieks and dives into a nearby bush. "Quick! Somepony hide me!"

"Rarity!" Charity cries, running over. "Are you all right?"

"*Shhh!*" Rarity hisses. After a few moments, she peeks her head out from the branches. "Is she gone?"

"Is who gone?" asks Rainbow Dash.

"Golden Harvest!" Rarity whispers. "I simply *cannot* see her!"

"What's wrong, sugarcube?" Applejack asks.

Rarity's lip quivers. "I'm supposed to deliver the Ponyville Choir costumes to her next week. But I..."

Pinkie Pie takes a deep breath. "But

you hate your design. You thought
having an apprentice would help, but
you're not sure how to teach her. So
now you're embarrassed because you
have no outfits and no clue what you're
doing?"

"Oh, Pinkie! It's
true!" Rarity
cries. "I have...
designer's block!"

Charity gasps.

"Charity, darling,

you might as well head home," Rarity sniffs. "I'm sure you don't want to stay now that you know I'm a failure!" Rarity sobs.

Charity blinks, then grins. "Forget my H.O.O.F. project! Let's go finish those dresses!"

"Really?" Rarity says, perking up. "You'll stay?"

"Of course!" Charity nods. "Like I always say: 'When the going gets tough, the tough get sewing!'"

Everypony laughs.

"Good one, Charity!" Pinkie Pie giggles.

Rarity narrows her eyes. What sort of pony takes credit for another pony's words? But she lets it go. She needs Charity's help.

"Well, in that case, let's go! We have work to do!" Rarity announces, then she trots off.

"We have work to do!" Charity echoes. "Rarity, wait up!"

Chapter 9

Rarity lifts up a finished dress. "Another one down!"

"Another one down!" echoes Charity, smiling. "Do you need anything else?" she asks eagerly.

"Some more tea? A back massage?"

Rarity sighs. She remembers Twilight's warning that Charity might be getting carried away in her admiration for Rarity. Maybe Rarity and Charity need to have some time apart.

Charity looks tired, and her mint-colored mane is becoming a little wild.

"Charity, you've done more than enough. Please go and do something fun!" Rarity passes Charity a list. "Just run these errands, and then the afternoon is yours."

"Are you sure?" Charity asks. "I could organize your fabrics again!"

"No, no! I won't hear another word about it. Go on, shoo!" Rarity pushes the pony out the door, then breathes a sigh of relief.

When Charity has run all the errands on Rarity's list, she wonders what to do with her free time.

She catches her reflection in a window as she passes. Her mane looks awfully frizzy. "An untidy mane equals a plain Jane, as Rarity would say." Something has to be done!

Suddenly, she notices a building with a purple roof. The sign out front has a picture of a mare with a beautiful, flowing mane and tail. Charity eagerly trots over. Maybe they can help with her bad mane day!

Inside, Charity is greeted by a pink

pony with a slicked-back blue mane.

"Welcome to La Ti Da Spa," she says.
"What can we do for you today?"

"I need something for my mane,"
says Charity. She smiles. Rarity is going
to be so impressed. "Do you ponies do
mane coloring here?"

Chapter 10

"**V**oilà!" Rarity announces as she finishes the final dress. "And I still have time for a hooficure before the choir costumes need to be delivered."

Rarity scribbles a note for Charity:

Dearest Charity,

Beauty emergency—I'll be back soon

to bring the outfits to the concert.

Hope you had fun around town!

xoxoxoxoxoxo,

Rarity

Charity arrives at the concert an hour before showtime, completely out of breath. The choir dresses were much heavier than she had guessed. But Rarity will be so proud that Charity has delivered them. And with her newly-dyed purple mane and tail, she looks just like her idol!

"I'm here! I'm here!" Charity shouts.

"Thank Celestia!" says Golden Harvest. She calls to the other choir members. "Rarity's here, everypony! Costume time!"

"Oh, I'm not Rar—" Charity starts to say, but she is interrupted.

"Wow, Rarity! You've really outdone yourself this time." Lyra Heartstrings hugs her dress. "I want to wear it every day!"

"Such attention to detail, Rarity!" adds Twinkleshine, admiring the expert hoofiwork.

Charity knows she shouldn't take the

credit, but it's wonderful to hear everypony singing her praises!

"Oh, thank you so much, everypony," Charity beams. "I just felt so ... inspired by your gorgeous voices!"

"They look stunning!" says Golden Harvest. "Say, Rarity, something's different about you. But I can't quite put my hoof on it."

Charity gives a nervous laugh and tosses her mane. "Whatever do you mean, darling?"

Chapter 11

Rarity stands in her boutique, sobbing uncontrollably. Her friends are with her, trying to calm her down. "The choir costumes have been stolen!" she howls in dismay. "All that hard work

down the drain. And my reputation—
ruined!"

"Are you sure?" asks Rainbow Dash.

"Yes, I'm sure!" Rarity sniffs. Where
is Charity when she needs a tissue?
"But I must face this like a true
professional," Rarity declares. "I must
go and tell Golden Harvest."

"Ten minutes to showtime, everypony!"
Rarity hears Golden Harvest call as she

arrives backstage.

Rarity smooths down her mane and takes a deep breath as she steps through the curtain.

"I regret to inform you all that there will be no costumes! They have been stolen," Rarity announces. "Please accept my deepest apologies."

Her words are met with giggles. The choir is standing in front of her, wearing their specially-designed outfits. But how?

"Rarity, you're a hoot!" says Twinkleshine, smoothing down her skirt.

"What? I thought that they..." Rarity says slowly. "Where did you get these?"

"You brought them, of course," says Golden Harvest.

"I did?" Rarity feels a bit faint. Is she losing her mind?

Tippy Tappy puts a hoof on her shoulder. "Rarity, are you okay?"

"I'm perfectly fine," Rarity lies,

backing away. On her way out, she hears somepony call her name.

"Yes?" Rarity says, peeking back through the curtain.

"Yes?" says another pony nearby at the same time. "Did somepony need something from *moi*, Rarity?"

"I just wondered if you could redo my bow tie, Rarity," a stallion asks the pony.

Rarity's eyes grow wide with shock.

The other pony giggles. "Anytime, darling!"

Rarity cranes her neck to get a better view and tumbles straight through the curtain into the back of the stage!

"Rarity!" Charity cries, running over to her. "Are you all right?"

All Rarity can see is purple. Is she looking into a mirror? No, she is looking at an imposter—Charity!

"Take off those wigs this instant!"

Rarity screeches.

"They aren't wigs." Charity looks down. "I dyed my mane and tail. I thought it would look fabulous."

"Well, it does," Rarity admits. "But only on me! Did you steal the choir costumes?!"

"No! I brought them over because you were running late," Charity explains. "I wanted to make sure your beautiful work arrived on time."

Rarity softens. "Oh. Well, you shouldn't do things like that without telling me first, okay?"

Charity nods as the show starts on the other side of the curtain. Rarity and Charity peek through the curtain to watch.

Golden Harvest steps forward. She twirls, and the beautiful dress billows out.

"My dresses are amazing!" Charity

says, completely mesmerized.

Rarity raises an eyebrow. She is beginning to wonder what sort of show Charity is putting on.

✷ Chapter 12 ✷

The next day, Rarity calls her friends for a secret meeting to ask for their help. "I'm afraid there is a crisis," Rarity tells them.

"What is it?" asks Applejack.

"Charity is trying to *steal my life*!" Rarity cries.

Twilight sighs. "This is what I was trying to tell you at the picnic. Charity thinks that if she copies you, she'll become the type of pony she looks up to."

"This is the worst possible thing!" Rarity moans. "How would Charity like it if somepony copied *her*?" Suddenly, Rarity has an idea. "Oh! That's it!" She races off.

"Wait! Where are you going?"
Rainbow Dash shouts after her.

"I'm just going to have to show
Charity how great it is to be herself,"
Rarity calls back.

Back in town, Rarity finds Charity with
Spike, searching for gems. She adjusts
her mint-colored wigs and smooths
down the light-green dress from
Charity's suitcase. She's ready.

"Here you are!" Rarity calls, trotting over with a grand flourish.

"Wow, Rarity!" Spike says. "You look amazing!"

"Hey! That's my design!" Charity cries. "And your mane! You dyed it?" Charity touches her own purple mane. "But I thought purple was in."

"I thought I'd try something new," Rarity explains. "You don't think it's fabulous?"

"Well, yes, but..." Charity says. "It's

like you're trying to look like me!"
Charity frowns. "Or how I used to
look...before I started trying to be you."
Charity slumps. "Oh."

Rarity smiles. "I can hardly blame
you for copying my style. But, Charity,
darling," she says, taking off the wigs,
"I would never dye my mane."

"Oh, Rarity, I'm so sorry!" Charity
exclaims. "I've been the worst
apprentice in all Equestria."

"I haven't been the best teacher,

either," Rarity admits.

"Are you kidding?" Charity exclaims. "This experience has been incredible. You're the greatest fashion designer of all time, Rarity."

Rarity gets a little choked up. "You're well on your way, too. This gown is simply stunning!"

Charity gives Rarity a hug. "Can we start over?"

"Absolutely!" Rarity sticks out her

hoof. "Hi, I'm Rarity."

"And I'm Sweetmint." Sweetmint laughs, head held high. "Want to go to the spa? I need to have my mane redone...."

"Only if we work on your fashion line after!" Rarity says.

"Deal!" Sweetmint nods.

Chapter 13

Sweetmint adjusts an aqua gown. "Does it look better now, Rarity?"

"Up a little higher on the left," Rarity says. "Make sure everypony can see the shells on the neckline."

Sweetmint adjusts the dress then steps back to look at it. Her "Sparkling Sea" fashion line is inspired by the magical world of Seaponies. The dresses are beautiful.

"I still can't believe we're here at Sacks! With a fashion line that I designed—I mean, that *we* designed." She giggles.

"No, darling, this was all you," Rarity says, smiling. "Personally, I think the inspiration came from all those

Bluedazzle berry tarts I made you eat."

Sweetmint winces. "Rarity, I have a confession," she says. "I absolutely *detest* Bluedazzle berries!"

"I know, darling," Rarity replies with a wink and a smile. "I know."